ANIMAL STARS
Midnight the Movie Star

Also in the Animal Stars series

ANIMAL STARS
Midnight the Movie Star

Narinder Dhami

Illustrated by Strawberrie Donnelly

Hodder
Children's
Books

a division of Hodder Headline plc

**With thanks to Gill Raddings of Stunt Dogs
for reviewing the film and animal training information
within this book.**

First published in Great Britain in 1999
by Hodder Children's Books

A Catalogue record for this book is available from the British Library

ISBN 0 340 74404 9

Typeset by Avon Dataset Ltd, Bidford-on-Avon, Warks

Printed and bound in Great Britain by
The Guernsey Press Co. Ltd, Channel Isles

Hodder Children's Books
a division of Hodder Headline
338 Euston Road
London NW1 3BH

1

"Hi, Albert!" Kim Miller dropped her schoolbag, and went over to the large cage in the corner of the living-room. "Are you going to say hello to me?"

Albert stared back at Kim with beady black eyes, ruffled his grey feathers and stayed stubbornly silent. Kim turned round and grinned at her best friend, Sarah Ramsay, and their classmate, Veronica Maxwell – Albert's owner.

"This is going to be a really difficult one!" Kim

said, raising her eyebrows. "Has he ever said *anything*, Ronnie?"

Veronica shook her head. "Not a sausage! He's an African Grey parrot as well, and they're supposed to be the best talkers. I just don't know why he won't speak!"

"He's gorgeous, though, isn't he?" said Sarah. Albert immediately preened himself, fluffing up his feathers and squawking, as if he knew exactly what they were saying. The three girls laughed.

"He's a real show-off!" said Ronnie, unlatching the cage. Albert immediately hopped out and on to her shoulder, pecking affectionately at a lock of Ronnie's long brown hair with his curved beak. "Have you got any ideas how I can get him to talk then, Kim?"

Kim frowned. As the animal expert on the school magazine, the *Hightown Herald*, she was often asked to solve a variety of problems which the other pupils were experiencing with their pets. Her mum and dad ran an agency called *Animal Stars*, which trained animals for all kinds of TV and media work, so Kim was used to handling animals and trying to solve their problems. She wanted to be an animal trainer herself when she grew up, so it was all good practice. Today she'd come over to the Maxwells' house after school to see if she could help Veronica with Albert.

"I suppose you're talking to him all the time?" she asked Ronnie, as Albert decided to take off and fly over to the top of the bookcase.

"Well, yes, when we're at home," Ronnie replied. "I'm at school all day and Mum and Dad both go out to work, but we talk to him in the evenings."

"Oh, right." Kim glanced over at Albert, then looked inside his cage. "It looks like he's been pulling a few of his feathers out. That probably means he gets a bit bored in the day when he's here on his own."

"That's what I thought," said Ronnie, looking worried. "But I don't know what to do about it. Mum won't let me have another bird to keep him company."

"You could try leaving the TV or the radio on for him when you're out," Kim suggested, flicking her long blonde fringe out of her eyes. "Then he'd be hearing people talking all day, and that might start him off."

Ronnie's eyes lit up as Albert swooped down

on to her shoulder again, and began pecking at his red tail feathers. "You think?"

Kim shrugged. "It's worth a try. Or you could record yourself talking into a cassette tape, and leave it running!"

Sarah laughed. "Or you could let him listen to a music tape, and then you'd have the only parrot in the world who can sing Spice Girls songs!"

"I'd be happy if he just said 'hello,' 'goodbye' and 'who's a pretty boy, then!' " said Ronnie with a grin.

"Hang on a sec, I've just thought of something else." Kim snapped her fingers. "There's some kind of little machine you can buy to help birds learn to talk. I remember my dad talking about it ages ago."

"What is it?" Ronnie looked interested.

"It's a bit like a tape recorder, but I think it switches on automatically whenever the bird makes a noise." Kim frowned, trying to remember the details. "You can record your own voice on it as well. I don't know how much it costs, though."

"Can you find out?" Ronnie asked eagerly.

Kim nodded. "I'll ask Dad." Then she glanced at her watch. "Come on, Sarah, we'd better get off home. 'Bye, Albert!" She reached out to stroke him, then had second thoughts, and glanced at Ronnie. "Does he bite?"

"Sometimes, if he's in a bad mood!" Ronnie grinned. "But he's usually all right if I'm with him."

" 'Bye then, Albert!" Kim scratched the parrot's head, and she and Sarah picked up their bags and left.

"I thought it was easy to teach parrots to talk," Sarah remarked as they walked down the Maxwells' path. She and Kim had been best friends for years, although they were opposites in many ways. Sarah was short and dark and took life pretty calmly, while Kim was tall and fair-haired and had an explosive temper which unfortunately often got the better of her. But they got on very well because they both had the same wacky sense of humour, and they both adored animals. Sarah loved hearing about *Animal Stars*, and the adventures Kim had when she was allowed to accompany her parents to a TV or film set.

"It *is* usually," Kim replied as they set off on the short walk out of the suburbs of the large city of

Highbridge, and into the countryside where they both lived. "I guess Albert just doesn't feel like learning at the moment!"

"Hey, slow down a bit!" Sarah scurried to keep up with Kim, who was walking along really fast. "My legs aren't as long as yours, you know!"

"Sorry." Kim waited for her friend to catch up. "I want to get home and find out if anything's happened about that *Animal Stars* job I told you about the other day."

"What, you mean the one your parents are keeping a secret?" Sarah puffed, out of breath already. "What do you reckon it is?"

Kim shrugged. "I don't know, but it must be something big because my mum's pretty excited about it! All I know is that some other animal trainer has dropped out at the last minute, so *Animal Stars* might be taking over."

"Is it a TV programme?" Sarah asked eagerly, "Or is it something else?" *Animal Stars* did mostly TV jobs, although they also trained animals for other types of work. Recently, Kim's mum had even trained some pedigree cats to take part in an important fashion show.

"I just don't know." Kim sounded frustrated.

"But I hope Mum tells me soon, or I'm going to burst!" She waved as Sarah turned down the lane which led to the cottage where the Ramsays lived. "See you tomorrow then."

" 'Bye!" Sarah called back, and ran off.

Kim continued on down the lane to the Millers' house. It stood on its own, surrounded by fields and with large gardens front and back, which were useful for training the animals. Kim went up to the front door, and let herself in with her key.

"I'm home!" she yelled, flinging her bag down in the hall. As usual, almost before the words were out of her mouth, there was a stampede of dogs from the kitchen. Harry and Spike charged towards Kim, barking uproariously, tails wagging, while Casper galloped along behind them. They all surged round Kim, licking her hands and sniffing at her trainers.

"Hello, hello, hello!" Kim laughed, patting each dog in turn. All three of the dogs were family pets, but they were also highly trained and experienced professionals. Harry, the Jack Russell, could perform many different tricks, and had already appeared in several TV programmes and commercials. Kim's parents were expecting even more work to come in for Harry when the new police drama *Coppers*, in which Harry had a starring role, went out on TV later that year. Spike, a cute shaggy mongrel who hadn't been with the Millers for very long, was already a star after appearing in two very popular soft drink commercials, and Casper, a gentle, good-natured Golden Retriever, was also in demand.

"Hi, you." Kim went into the kitchen, where her older brother Luke was sitting at the table, head bent over his homework.

"Hi." Luke didn't look up.

"Where's Mum?" Kim went over to the biscuit tin and grabbed a handful of chocolate biscuits, while the dogs milled around her legs eagerly, hoping for a crumb.

"In the office," Luke replied, still writing busily. "And Dad's out on a job with those owls."

"Oh, yeah, the building society commercial." Kim held her biscuits out of reach of the three dogs and peered over Luke's shoulder. "Has Mum said anything else about this top secret thing that she's working on?"

"Nope," Luke said briefly. "Shut up, will you? I want to get this homework finished."

"Why? Are you going out with *Lucy* tonight?" Kim asked in her most annoying voice. She still couldn't get over the fact that Luke was interested in girls, and what was even more puzzling, that girls were interested in him. She also secretly resented the fact that although they'd always been close when they were younger, now that Luke was a teenager, they didn't seem to be able to hold a conversation any more without it turning into a full-on argument.

"Yeah, I am," Luke said shortly.

Kim shrugged, and poured herself a glass of lemonade. She was just wondering whether to go and start her own homework, when her mum came out of the large study adjoining the kitchen which served as the *Animal Stars* office.

"Hi, Kim." Rachel Miller looked very similar to her daughter, with the same blonde hair and blue eyes, but Kim had inherited her father's height and long legs, while her mother was much shorter and more petite. "Had a good day at school? How did you get on with the Maxwells' parrot?"

"All right." Kim grinned. "I reckon Albert's intelligent enough to talk if he wants to, he just doesn't want to yet!"

9

"I'm sure that's true," her mum replied. "I remember reading that African Greys aren't just good mimics, they can actually understand and use human language correctly!"

"Really?" Kim looked interested.

Her mum nodded. "There's probably plenty of stuff about parrots on the Net. You should take a look some time."

"Yeah, good idea." Kim grabbed her glass of lemonade, and headed towards the *Animal Stars* office. "Is it OK if I use the computer right now, Mum?"

"Not at the moment, no." Rachel Miller shook her head. "I'm expecting some important calls in the next few minutes, and I need to have access to the computer files."

"Important calls?" Kim's ears immediately pricked up. "Is it about this top secret job you won't tell us about?"

"It isn't top-secret, Kim!" her mother said with a smile. "You know I don't like talking about work until everything's fixed for definite."

"And is it definite now?" Kim asked eagerly.

Her mum hesitated, then nodded slowly. "Yes, I think it is!"

10

"Well, what is it then?" Kim demanded excitedly, and all the dogs started jumping around her, barking, obviously wondering what was going on. "Oh, come on, Mum, you can tell us now, can't you?"

"I was going to wait till your dad got home," Rachel Miller began with a twinkle in her eyes, but Kim groaned loudly.

"Oh, *Mum*!"

"Tell her, Mum, *please*!" Luke muttered, throwing his pen down on to the table, "Or she'll *never* shut up!"

"Well, it's pretty exciting really," said Kim's mum with a beaming smile. "*Animal Stars* has just landed its first Hollywood movie!"

"*What?*! Oh, that's so cool!" Kim squealed, almost dropping the glass of lemonade in her excitement. "What's the film? Who's in it?"

"Does that mean you're going to America?" Luke chimed in, almost as excited as Kim was.

"Which animals are going to be in it?"

"Can we come to America too?"

"Quiet!" Rachel Miller clapped her hands over her ears, and looked sternly at the three dogs. Immediately they all stopped barking, and sat

down to attention. "Nobody's going to America. The part of the movie that *Animal Stars* is involved in is being filmed in Wales."

"Wales!" Luke snorted in disgust. "I thought I was going to get the chance to go to LA!"

"Who's in the film, Mum?" Kim asked again, "What's it about?"

"It's called *The Shadow of the Horse*, it's set in Victorian times, and it's based around a real legend about the ghost of a black horse that's supposed to roam the Welsh valleys, helping people who are in trouble," Kim's mother told her. "I've seen the script. It's quite scary in parts!"

"It sounds a bit boring to me!" Luke remarked.

"Well, there are no car chases or bombs or alien spaceships!" his mum said dryly. "But it has got Melissa Murray and Cameron Bond in it, so it will probably be a big hit."

"Melissa Murray!" gasped Kim, her eyes round. Melissa Murray was one of the most famous film stars in Hollywood, and Kim had already seen the beautiful actress once before. She had been in the audience at the fashion show Kim had attended with her mum and the pedigree cats a month or so ago. Cameron Bond was a young up-and-coming star too.

"Cameron's not in the Welsh sequences, so only Melissa Murray will be filming over here," Kim's mum went on. "It's all happening really quickly too, because the original trainer who was hired dropped out at the last minute."

"So it's *Animal Stars* to the rescue!" said Kim with a grin. "Which horse are you going to use, Mum?"

"Well, as you know we've got a couple of black horses on the agency books," her mum replied. "But after a lot of discussion, we've gone for Midnight."

"Oh, great! Midnight's lovely!" Kim exclaimed. She'd met the sleek, graceful horse, who was owned by a family who lived in Scotland, when Midnight had been trained by Rachel Miller to take part in a TV commercial.

"He's well-trained too," Kim's mum said with a grin, "Even if I do say so myself! He should be capable of doing everything in the script with very little additional training."

"I can't wait for filming to start!" Kim said eagerly. She usually found all the work *Animal Stars* did really exciting, but this was different. She couldn't wait to tell Sarah. A big Hollywood movie! And with any luck, she'd be allowed to go to some of the filming, like she usually did.

"Yes, well, it's only a month or two away and I've got lots of stuff to do before then," her mother sighed. "I'm going to be away filming for two weeks from just after Easter, so I've got to make sure your dad can cope here on his own."

"So when can we come to watch?" Kim asked eagerly. Sometimes she really hated school for getting in the way of her going out on jobs with her parents, but at least there were weekends, and Wales wasn't too far away, not as far as America!

MIDNIGHT THE MOVIE STAR

Her mum looked at her, and this time she wasn't smiling. "Kim, I think we need to talk about that," she said.

2

Kim felt as if someone had chucked a bucket of cold water over her as she saw the look on her mother's face.

"What's up?" she asked with a frown. "I *will* be able to come and watch some of the filming, won't I? I know it's a bit difficult with school and everything."

"Kim, I don't think it's a good idea this time," her mum said gently.

"Uh-oh!" said Luke under his breath. "Time for

fireworks!"

Kim glared at him, then turned back to her mother. "But, Mum, I really want to see Melissa Murray working with Midnight! I've never seen a Hollywood movie being filmed before!"

"Neither have I," her mother pointed out, "And that's why I need to be right on the ball for this job. This could be a big break for *Animal Stars*, and I have to make sure everything goes perfectly."

"But I wouldn't get in the way," Kim began desperately.

"I said no, Kim, and I mean it," her mother said. "With this all coming at such short notice, I can't afford any mistakes and you do have a tendency to get a bit too involved when things get sticky!"

Kim turned pink. She usually kept a very low profile when she was allowed to go on set with her parents, but several times in the not-so-distant past she'd just *had* to interfere when something had gone wrong! Usually things turned out for the best, but her mum obviously wasn't going to take any chances this time.

"I could come just for a weekend," she suggested hopefully, but still her mum shook her head.

"No, Kim. Now, what do you want for tea, you two?"

"Tough luck, Kimmy," Luke said as Kim slumped down disconsolately on to the chair next to him.

"It's not fair!" Kim muttered. "My first Hollywood movie, and I'm not allowed to go!"

"Well, you heard what Mum said." Luke picked up his pen again. "She reckons that if this goes well, they might get more work from Hollywood."

"Huh! It's still not fair!" Kim groaned, kicking at the table leg. She'd never felt so disappointed in her whole life.

"So it's *Animal Stars'* first Hollywood movie," Kim announced gloomily, "And I'm not even allowed to go!"

"That's terrible!" Sarah sympathised. "Can't you try and change your mum's mind?"

"Nah, she's got that look in her eye which means I can ask till I'm blue in the face and I won't get!" Kim muttered, hiking her schoolbag further up on to her shoulder. It was the following morning, and the two girls had met up as usual to walk to school. "So I haven't got a hope."

"Poor you," Sarah said as they walked up the lane towards the main road which led into Highbridge. "I guess your mum just wants things to go right because it's such an important job."

"Yeah, I know," Kim sighed. "She doesn't want me interfering if things go wrong!"

"You don't interfere!" Sarah said loyally.

"Well, I do. Sort of." Kim grinned reluctantly. "But I'm only trying to help!"

"Yeah, do you remember all that trouble with Jamie Marshall and Casper?" Sarah reminded her. "We *both* nearly got into big grief over that!"

"But we got it sorted in the end though, didn't we?" Kim pointed out as they walked up to the gates of Hightown Primary. When Casper had appeared in several episodes of the popular soap *North Park Avenue*, one of its child stars, Jamie Marshall, had played endless tricks on the patient Golden Retriever. Kim and Sarah had been the only ones who had noticed, and they'd managed to put a stop to it.

"Oh, well, don't worry about it." Sarah slapped Kim on the back as they went into the playground. "If this goes well, *Animal Stars* is bound to get more film work, and then you might get a chance to go."

"Maybe." Kim pulled a face and nudged Sarah as Charlotte Appleby and her best mate Rosie Randall walked into the playground. "Don't say anything about it in front of Charlotte, OK? I'll never hear the end of it if she finds out *Animal Stars* are doing a Hollywood movie, and I'm not allowed to go to the filming!"

Tall, dark-haired Charlotte was in the same class as Kim, but they'd never really got on. Recently things had worsened between them after Charlotte had got Kim into serious trouble with her parents, which had almost resulted in her losing the chance to appear in a TV commercial with Spike. Charlotte pretended not to be at all interested in *Animal Stars*, but deep down she was secretly jealous of Kim's showbiz connections.

"Hey, Kim! What was that you were saying about a Hollywood movie?" yelled a loud voice behind Kim and Sarah. Kim spun round sharply to find Scott Brennan and Dean Jackson, two boys in her class, staring at her eagerly.

"Shut up!" Kim hissed. But it was too late. Charlotte Appleby's ears were already flapping, even though she was pretending not to be interested.

"What's the film about?" Scott went on, ignoring the warning look Kim was giving him.

"Yeah, who's in it?" Dean chimed in. "Anyone famous?"

"It's about a horse," Kim muttered, conscious of Charlotte and Rosie eavesdropping like mad.

"A horse?" Scott looked faintly disgusted. "Is it a cowboy movie then?"

"No, it's a ghost story and some of it's being shot in Wales," Kim said reluctantly. "Melissa Murray's in it."

The two boys looked a bit more impressed.

"Hey, did you hear that, Charlie?" Rosie Randall elbowed her friend in the ribs. "Melissa Murray! You like her, don't you?"

"She's OK," Charlotte said in a freezing voice, and tried to pull her away. But Rosie never could take a hint, however big. She was known throughout the school as Dozy Rosie.

"You're really lucky, Kim," Rosie said enviously. "Are you going to the filming?"

Kim was caught. She glanced desperately at Sarah. "I might," she said, trying to sound casual.

"Oh, you don't sound too sure." Charlotte moved in smoothly like a snake for the kill, sensing that something was going on. "You *are* allowed to go, aren't you, Kim?"

"I'm not sure yet," Kim mumbled.

"I bet your mum and dad don't want you messing everything up, that's why you're not allowed to go!" Charlotte said gleefully. Kim tried not to react, but the look on her face told Charlotte she'd hit the nail on the head. "They can't trust you to behave yourself!"

Kim saw red. "You don't know what you're talking about!" she snapped.

"Yes, so shut up, Charlotte!" Sarah cut in sharply, and she grabbed Kim's arm and bundled her off across the playground before things got out of hand.

"That's it!" Kim groaned. "Now she'll keep going on and on about it, and drive me mad!"

"Just ignore her," Sarah advised, without much hope.

"Hi, Kim, hi, Sarah." Ronnie Maxwell came across the playground towards them.

"Oh, hello, Ronnie," said Kim, calming down a bit. "Any luck with Albert yet?"

"Well, I've left the radio on for him today!" Ronnie said with a grin. "Maybe he'll say something when I get home!"

Kim turned to Sarah as Ronnie went off to join her friends. "Just my luck! My mum gets to meet Melissa Murray, and I'm stuck with a parrot who won't speak!"

"Right, you two, be good!" Rachel Miller hugged Kim, then Luke. "I've got a few days off in the middle of filming, so I'll pop back home in the next couple of weeks or so. And I'll ring as often as I can."

"We'll be fine, Mum," Luke said impatiently. "Don't fuss!"

"Yeah, Mum, we'll be fine," Kim said bravely. It was Saturday and her mum was leaving for Wales to start rehearsing for *The Shadow of the Horse*. Even though she'd had plenty of time to get used to the fact that she wasn't going to be allowed to go, Kim was still feeling pretty bad about it. Midnight's owners had brought the black horse down to Highbridge a few days before, and he had been staying at a local stables which was run by a couple called Lucy and John Hartwell, who were friends of the Millers. Kim's mum had driven over in the *Animal Stars* van with the horse-trailer on the back to collect Midnight, and the rest of the family had accompanied her in the car to say goodbye.

"Don't worry, love, I'll make sure they don't get into any mischief!" said Chris Miller, Kim's father, with a twinkle in his eye.

"Well, we'd better get going then." Rachel Miller glanced round the stables courtyard, just as tall, fair-haired Lucy Hartwell, dressed in shirt and jodhpurs, came towards them, leading Midnight alongside her.

"Here he is!" she said with a smile. "All ready to go!"

Midnight was a beautiful horse, with a coal-black, glossy coat, a well-shaped head, a flowing mane and tail, and long, elegant legs. He stepped proudly across the courtyard next to Lucy, tossing his head in welcome and taking a good look at everyone who was standing waiting for him.

"Hello, Midnight!" Kim said. She had a sugar-lump in her hand, ready for him. "Say hello!"

Midnight immediately lifted his right leg up, and Kim took his hoof and shook it. Then

MIDNIGHT THE MOVIE STAR

she gave him the sugar-lump.

"Is that a trick you taught him, Rachel?" said Lucy Hartwell with a grin.

Kim's mum nodded. "Yes, he's got a few more like that up his sleeve too!"

Kim patted Midnight's glossy neck. "Will he be doing tricks like that in the movie, Mum?"

"No, he's supposed to be a wild horse, so mostly he's galloping over the hills or appearing out of the mist, looking ghostly!" her mum replied. Filming of *The Shadow of the Horse* wouldn't actually be starting for a week or so which would give Kim's mum time to introduce Midnight to the actors, and settle the horse into his new role. Again Kim desperately wished that she was going too.

"I'm sure he'll be great, whatever he's doing," said Lucy Hartwell. "He's a real star – and he knows it!"

It took a little while to get Midnight settled comfortably in his horse-box, and then it was time for Kim's mum to leave.

" 'Bye, everyone!" she called as she pulled out of the stables. "I'll ring tonight to let you know I've arrived safely."

" 'Bye, Mum," Kim called, trying hard to swallow the lump in her throat. She watched until the van and the horse-box had disappeared down the road, and then sighed.

"Come on, love, cheer up." Kim's dad slipped an arm round her shoulders as they said goodbye to Lucy and went back to the car. "There'll be other films, hopefully, and other chances for you to visit the set."

"Yeah, I know," Kim muttered.

"And anyway, Albert needs you!" Luke said with a wicked grin.

Kim groaned. "Don't remind me! I've been going round to Ronnie's house every week for ages now, and Albert just won't say anything!"

"Maybe he's just the strong, silent type!" her father said solemnly.

"I'm going to get him to speak if it kills me!" Kim said in a determined voice. At least it would give her something to do until her mum got back, she thought gloomily.

Kim was on tenterhooks all day, waiting for her mum to phone. She was dying to know what was going on, and if her mum had met Melissa Murray yet. When the call finally came through that evening, Kim was sitting at the kitchen table with Sarah, playing Monopoly. As soon as the phone rang, Kim jumped up from her seat so fast she upset the playing-board, and all the pieces toppled off on to the floor.

"Hey, watch out!" said Sarah crossly.

"Never mind, I don't want to play any more!" Kim yelled over her shoulder as she lunged for the phone.

"Yeah, just because I was winning!" Sarah pointed out. "I had hotels on Mayfair *and* Park Lane!"

"Hello?" Kim grabbed the receiver.

"Hello, Kim!"

"Mum! How's things? Is Midnight OK? Have you met Melissa Murray yet?"

"Everything's fine!" her mother laughed. "I'm staying in a lovely hotel, and Midnight's being put up in a very nice stables, close to where we'll be doing most of the filming."

"And what about Melissa Murray?" Kim asked again eagerly. "Have you seen her yet?"

"Yes, she arrived this afternoon," her mum replied. "She's brought her daughter Caitlin over from the States with her. She's the same age as you."

"Oh." Kim immediately felt disgruntled. If Caitlin Murray was allowed to miss school to go to the filming, why couldn't *she*?

"I feel sorry for the poor girl," Kim's mum went on. "She's got a kind of governess with her called Mrs Franklin, who's a real dragon."

"Is that your mum?" Kim's father came out of the office.

Kim nodded. "Mum, Dad wants to talk to you. I'll speak to you later." And she handed the receiver over to her father.

"What's up with you?" Sarah asked as Kim went back to the table. "You've got a face on you like I don't know what."

"Mum says Melissa Murray's daughter's there to watch the filming," said Kim, pulling a face. "She's the same age as us, too."

"Well, why isn't she at school then?" Sarah asked.

"Oh, Caitlin's got a *governess*!" said Kim, putting on a posh voice.

Sarah giggled. "It must be weird having a film star for a mum! What do you think this Caitlin's like?"

"Oh, she probably thinks she's *it*!" Kim said scornfully. "I bet she wears designer clothes and has her own phone in her bedroom! That kind of thing."

"I bet she's pretty too," said Sarah. "Just like her mum."

"Yeah, and I bet she gets everything she wants," Kim said enviously.

"Oh, Mummy, I simply *must* have my own mobile phone and my own Jacuzzi and my own private swimming-pool!" Sarah drawled in quite a good imitation of an American accent.

The two girls fell about laughing. But Kim secretly still felt annoyed that Caitlin Murray was allowed to visit the movie set, while she was stuck in boring old school. It really wasn't fair at all.

"Albert, please, please, *please* speak to me!" Kim pleaded, staring through the bars of the parrot's cage. But Albert simply chewed on a sunflower seed, and stared back at her silently and triumphantly.

"Maybe he'll never say anything," said Ronnie, who was sitting on the Maxwells' sofa with Sarah. "We've tried everything. We've left the radio or the TV on every day for the last month while we've been out."

"Doesn't seem to have made much difference, does it?" Sarah remarked.

"Well, we're not giving up yet!" Kim said. She looked into the cage, and smiled encouragingly at the grey parrot. "Who's a pretty boy then?"

"Who's a pretty *quiet* boy, you mean, don't you?" Sarah said with a grin.

"By the time my mum gets back from Wales, this bird's going to be talking!" Kim vowed, shaking her head in disgust. "I'll come over again this weekend, Ronnie. We've got Monday off school because of the Bank Holiday, so we'll have plenty of time to work on Albert!"

"How's the filming going, by the way?" Ronnie asked, looking interested.

"OK, I think," Kim replied. "Mum's been away for almost two weeks now, but she phones us every so often to tell us all the gossip!"

"How's Midnight doing?" Sarah asked.

"He's doing brilliantly!" Kim said proudly. "Mum said he's going to be the star of the film!"

Just then the Maxwells' phone rang, and Ronnie went over to answer it.

"Hello?" She looked surprised, and then held

31

the receiver out to Kim. "Kim, it's for you – it's your mum!"

"My mum!" Kim repeated, looking surprised. Why on earth was her mum calling her at Ronnie's house? Puzzled, she took the receiver.

"Hello, Mum? What's going on?"

"Hi, Kim!" Rachel Miller sounded both pleased and slightly harassed at the same time. "I called home and your dad told me you were at Ronnie's and gave me the number. I've got a surprise for you!"

"What?" Kim asked eagerly.

"Well, I was talking to Melissa Murray today, and when she found out I had a daughter the same age as Caitlin, she asked me if you'd like to visit the set this weekend as her guest. She thinks Caitlin would like the company." Kim's mum paused, waiting for Kim's reaction. "What do you say? Would you like to come?"

Kim was so thrilled, she could hardly speak. "Of course I want to come!" she stammered. Even if she had to put up with snobby Caitlin Murray, she wouldn't miss this chance for anything!

"I thought you might say that!" laughed her mum. "It's all very short notice, so you'll need to pack tonight, and your dad will drive you here tomorrow afternoon. You'll need to leave school early, so your father's going to ring your headteacher, and square it with her."

"Brilliant!" Kim said breathlessly. She could hardly believe her luck. After all that disappointment, she was going to the movie set after all! She said goodbye to her mum, and then spun round to face Sarah and Ronnie, eyes shining.

"Mum says I can go and watch the filming this weekend! Isn't it *brilliant*!"

"BRILLIANT!" squawked a loud voice behind them, before Sarah and Ronnie could say a word.

The three girls all looked amazed. They stared at Albert the parrot with their mouths open.

"Albert!" Ronnie squealed. "You spoke! You spoke!"

"At last!" Kim sighed. Now she could go off and really enjoy herself, knowing that Albert was finally beginning to talk!

"Brilliant, brilliant, brilliant!" said Albert, and he strutted round his cage, looking very self-important.

3

"You're so lucky, Kim!" Sarah said enviously as they walked to school the following morning. "I wish I could come with you."

"I wish you could come too," said Kim. "But I'll tell you all about it when I get back."

"Anyway, at least you'll have Caitlin Murray to talk to!" said Sarah with a sly grin. "You two are going to be big mates!"

"I don't think so!" Kim snorted. "She'll probably turn her nose up at me because I haven't got loads of designer clothes or something!"

"Oh, well, who cares about her anyway!" said Sarah, as they walked into the playground. "You'll have a great time!"

"Hey, Kim!" Ronnie came running over to them, looking very excited. "You'll never guess what's happened – Albert's started saying other words now! We just can't stop him talking!"

"That's great, Ronnie," Kim said.

"And you know what?" Ronnie went on. "Last night he even started imitating the phone ringing. Mum kept jumping up to answer it until she realised it was Albert!"

"I bet by the time I come back he's started saying sentences!" said Kim confidently.

"I know, he's so clever, isn't he?" Ronnie said, beaming with pride. "Have a good time at the film set, Kim."

"I will," Kim assured her as the younger girl went off to join her mates.

"Whew, that was close!" Sarah grinned. "I thought Albert was going to be the animal agony aunt's first big failure!"

"Me too," Kim admitted. "I don't think I helped that much really. I reckon Albert knew exactly what he was doing all the time!"

"Oh, look, it's Kim!" Charlotte Appleby said silkily as she sauntered into the playground with Rosie by her side as usual. "How's the Hollywood movie going then? Oh, I forgot, you're not allowed to go, are you? What a shame!"

Kim grinned at Sarah. "Are you going to tell her, or shall I?"

"Tell me what?" Charlotte said sharply.

"That Melissa Murray's invited me to visit the set as her guest this weekend!" Kim said breezily.

"What? I don't believe you!" Charlotte snapped.

"It's true!" Sarah chimed in triumphantly. "She's asked Kim over to meet her daughter, Caitlin!"

"Is that true, Kim?" Rosie gasped, her eyes as round as saucers.

Kim nodded. "Yup, and I'm leaving school early this afternoon so that my dad can drive me to Wales." She glanced at Charlotte who was looking completely sour-faced. "So there you go!"

Looking very annoyed indeed, Charlotte turned on her heel, and stalked off, dragging Rosie along behind her. "I bet Melissa Murray's daughter doesn't like you anyway!" she snapped over her shoulder.

"One up to me, I think!" said Kim and she held up her hand for a high five from Sarah. "I enjoyed that!"

"It served Charlotte right!" said Sarah cheerfully.

Kim frowned. "Yeah, but I reckon Charlotte's right about one thing. I don't think Caitlin Murray and I are going to like each other one little bit."

"I can't believe I'm really going!" Kim said ecstatically as she buckled her seatbelt. "How long will it take to get there, Dad?"

"A few hours," her father replied, looking right and left before swinging the family estate car out of the school car park. "Your mum will still be working when we get there, so I'll take you straight to the set."

"Excellent!" Kim said, bouncing up and down in her seat. Her father had picked her up from school just after lunch when the rest of the class had been settling down to silent reading. Kim couldn't help smiling when she remembered the look on Charlotte's face as she'd said goodbye to Sarah and left the classroom! Chris Miller had brought Kim's small suitcase with him so that they could head straight off down the motorway.

"Did Mum ring this morning?" Kim asked as the car picked up speed.

"Yep, she just wanted to check that the school agreed to let you leave early," her father replied. He shot a sideways look at Kim. "She's in a bit of a flap, although she's looking forward to seeing you. You know how important it is that everything goes well for *Animal Stars*, don't you?"

Kim nodded. "I'm not going to do anything silly, Dad, if that's what you mean!"

"I know." Her father grinned at her. "But don't try to be too helpful either!"

"What a cheek!" Kim said indignantly, and her father laughed.

"Just have a good time, OK?"

"I will," Kim said confidently, although she couldn't help remembering all the things she and Sarah had said about Caitlin Murray. Maybe they'd been a bit mean, but if Caitlin did go around acting like a snob, just because her mum was a film star, Kim didn't intend to put up with it for a minute! "Dad," she asked diffidently, "Did Mum say anything to you about Caitlin Murray?"

"Melissa's daughter?" Kim's father steered the

car into the fast lane of the motorway. "No, not really, except that Caitlin was very quiet."

"Quiet!" Kim repeated with a frown. That didn't sound right. Oh, well, it wouldn't be long before she'd find out for herself exactly what Caitlin Murray was like . . .

The journey seemed to take ages, and Kim soon got bored. She asked her father so many times if they were nearly there yet that he put the radio on to drown her out. Then Kim started to feel drowsy, and her eyes began to close. She woke up with a start over an hour later and sat up.

"Dad, are we in Wales now?"

"Looks like it!" her father said with a grin.

Kim stared out of the window. The scenery had magically changed while she was asleep. Instead of mile after mile of boring, concrete motorway, there were sheep and lambs grazing on the green hills and the valleys, and fresh, clean air was blowing in through the open car window.

"Are we nearly there, Dad?" Kim asked eagerly.

"Yes, at last!" her father replied, rolling his eyes. "We're about twenty minutes from the set. They're filming on some private farmland to keep the public out."

Kim watched eagerly as her father drove along the winding road around the hillside, eventually drawing up at a bumpy track which led off to one side. A group of security men with walkie-talkies were patrolling the entrance to the track, and they checked out who Kim and her father were, before letting them pass. Then they bumped their way down the track, which led them down into the valley.

"Here we are, Kim." Her father nodded at the scene laid out in front of them. "This is the area where they're doing most of the filming."

Kim had been on several outdoor sets when she'd visited TV programmes which were being filmed on location, but this was on a much bigger scale, as befitted a Hollywood production. There seemed to be more of everything – more equipment, more lights and more people rushing busily about. The film company had erected some grey stone cottages especially for the film, and although they looked very old and very realistic, Kim knew that the buildings were just shells, and would only be used for the external shots. Any scenes inside the cottages would be filmed on studio sets, probably back in the States. To one side, well away from the cottages, was a lake, and there seemed to be quite a lot of activity going on over there.

"There's Mum!" Kim nudged her dad as she spotted Rachel Miller down by the water. "And Midnight!"

"Looks like they're rehearsing a scene," her father said as he parked the car next to the film crew's vehicles. "Let's take a walk down there and see what's going on."

Kim jumped out of the car, shaking with excitement. She could hardly believe her eyes when suddenly she spotted a very familiar figure standing down by the lake, amongst all the cameras and crew.

"Dad!" Kim tugged at her father's sleeve as they moved closer to the scene of the action. "That's Melissa Murray!"

There was no mistaking Melissa Murray's flowing red curls and tall, elegant figure, even though she was dressed in a rather drab grey, Victorian dress and flat shoes. Kim watched eagerly as Melissa stood very still and was fussed over by the hair, make-up and wardrobe people who ran around her, adjusting a stray lock of hair, powdering her nose and straightening her dress. The actress also had a very realistic-looking bruise painted on to her left temple, from which a tiny trickle of fake blood was flowing.

"Right, can we run through that scene again?" called a woman with short blonde hair and enormous silver glasses, whom Kim guessed was probably one of the assistant directors. "Curtis wants to get this in the can today if possible."

"Who's Curtis?" Kim whispered to her father.

"Curtis Bernard, the director," her father told her. "There he is, up there."

The director, a big, plump bear of a man with a shaggy beard, was sitting on a chair on top of a platform so that he could get a better view of what was going on.

"Let's try and get this right, people!" he roared, eyeballing everyone underneath it. "The light's going to be just perfect for a take very soon."

Kim could see her mother and Midnight standing quietly beside the lake. Kim knew her mum had spotted them, but she was too professional to wave or call out, and Kim didn't wave either. She knew better than to interrupt her mum at work, especially when a scene was about to be rehearsed.

Melissa was led over to the side of the lake by another of the assistant directors, and Kim saw that there were marks on the grass to guide the actress into position. Melissa Murray lay down on the grass, and sprawled out very still as if unconscious after some sort of accident. Meanwhile Kim saw her mother focusing Midnight's attention on Melissa lying on the ground directly in front of them.

The rehearsal began. After a few seconds, Kim's mother released Midnight and told him to "touch". The black horse moved slowly forward and nosed at Melissa Murray's hair. After a second or two Melissa sat up with a gasp, and stared at the horse as if she couldn't believe her eyes. Right on his cue from Rachel Miller, Midnight pawed the ground a few times. Then, as Melissa Murray stretched out a tentative hand to touch the animal, a quick word from Kim's mother made Midnight wheel round and trot back towards her.

"Excellent! That looked great!" Curtis Bernard called approvingly.

"Right, we're going for a take!" shouted the

woman in the silver glasses. "Are those dry ice machines working properly now?"

Kim watched with interest as everyone bustled around while the assistant directors yelled orders and Curtis Bernard sat back in his chair, keeping an eye on everything that was going on. Melissa Murray was once again being fussed around by three or four people, while Midnight was standing patiently by chewing on a small piece of carrot Kim's mum had given him as a reward for performing well.

Within a very few minutes the scene had been set up again, and the large dry ice machines had been turned on. Plumes of misty white smoke were now drifting around Melissa and Midnight and curling out over the lake, carefully controlled so that the effect of a misty evening was obtained without obscuring the actress and the horse from view. As silence fell, a young woman with pink and purple streaked hair slapped her clapperboard smartly together and called "Scene 41, take 1!"

Kim could tell that this time the scene would look a lot more atmospheric with all the mist drifting and curling around Melissa and Midnight in the dying sunlight. She didn't realise that she was holding her breath as she watched them do the scene until the director said "Cut! That was perfect for a first take!", and everyone on the set burst into spontaneous applause.

That scene wrapped up the filming for the day, and Kim and her father immediately hurried over to Rachel and Midnight.

"Hi Mum!" Kim hugged her mother enthusiastically, and then patted Midnight, who tossed his head and nuzzled at her shoulder. "Wasn't Midnight fab?"

"He certainly was," her mother agreed. "He's done everything right so far." She glanced at her husband and smiled. "Everything's going really well."

"Glad to hear it," said Chris Miller. "Look, I can stay for a quick bite to eat and then I've got to get back."

"All right, let's go over to the catering trailer then," Kim's mum began, and then stopped as she saw someone coming towards them. "Oh, Melissa! This is my daughter, Kim."

"I thought it must be." Melissa Murray smiled her famous smile at Kim, and held out her hand.

Her heart hammering with excitement, Kim took it and smiled back. Melissa Murray was even more beautiful in real life than she appeared on the screen, with very white, creamy skin and large green eyes. "Nice to meet you, honey."

"Nice to meet you too," Kim stammered.

"And here's my little Caitlin to say hello to you," said Melissa. She looked round and Kim saw a large, grim-faced woman dressed in a severe black suit ushering an awkward-looking, skinny girl towards them. The girl was very pale, and she had lanky brown hair and braces on her teeth.

46

She wore faded and frayed jeans and an old sweatshirt.

Kim just about stopped herself falling over in amazement. *This* was the rich and beautiful Caitlin Murray?

4

"I didn't know Melissa Murray's daughter was going to look like that!" Kim muttered as her mum pulled away from the car park, Midnight safely tucked away in the horse-box behind them. Kim's father had already left to begin the long drive back to Highbridge.

"What do you mean?" her mum asked, and there was a note in her voice that told Kim she'd better be careful what she said.

"Well, I thought she'd be sort of beautiful like

her mum," Kim said cautiously. "And I thought she'd be wearing designer clothes and all that. You know."

"Caitlin seems perfectly nice, although she's a bit shy," her mum replied. "She seems a bit young for her age too."

Oh, great, Kim groaned inwardly. I've been landed with a right one here! But she knew better than to say anything like that to her mother. Maybe Caitlin would turn out to be OK, after all. At least she wasn't going to laugh at Kim for not wearing expensive designer clothes, which was what Kim had secretly been worried about.

"Her tutor's a bit scary!" she said with a grin. "She looks like she could crush an iron bar with her bare hands!"

"I know, she does look a bit grim!" her mother agreed, and they both giggled. "They're staying in the same hotel as us, so you'll probably have time to get to know Caitlin a bit better tonight."

"Oh, good," said Kim, trying to sound enthusiastic. Ahead of them she could see a cluster of buildings and a group of children on ponies having a riding lesson in a nearby field. "Is this where Midnight's staying?"

"Yes, this is Greyfriars Stables." Kim's mum pulled up and turned off the engine. "That's Tom Grayson, who owns this place."

Tom Grayson, a tall, dark-haired man in his early forties, was hurrying across the courtyard towards them. Meanwhile, some of the horses in the stables around the yard were craning their necks curiously over the stable doors to see what was going on.

"Hello, Rachel. And this must be Kim." He grinned at her and Kim smiled back. "How did Midnight get on today?"

"He was perfect!" Kim's mum replied as she went round to open the horse box. "Didn't put a foot wrong!"

"Right, well, he deserves a good meal now then!" said Tom cheerfully.

Kim watched as her mum and Tom Grayson expertly released Midnight from the horse-box and led him over to his stable. Then a clatter of hooves caught her attention, and the group of children whom Kim had seen riding across the field trotted into the yard.

"Do you ride, Kim?" Tom called as he unlatched the stable door and led Midnight inside.

"No, I've never learnt," Kim called back.

"Well, you could take a few lessons while you're here if you like," Tom suggested. "We've always got a spare pony or two hanging about."

Kim's eyes lit up. "But I'm only here for the weekend."

Tom shrugged. "That's long enough to tell whether you like it or not! And if you do, maybe you can carry on when you go home."

"Can I, Mum?" Kim asked breathlessly.

"I don't see why not," her mother laughed. "Midnight and I aren't involved in the filming tomorrow afternoon, so you could have your first lesson then."

"Great!" Kim said eagerly. She rushed over to say goodbye to Midnight, and then climbed back into the car. She was going to have a good time this weekend, Kim told herself happily, even if Caitlin Murray *did* turn out to be a big wet drip!

"Hey, Mum, do you think Caitlin might want to come riding with me?" she asked suddenly, feeling a bit guilty about thinking rude things about the other girl. After all, Kim had hardly even spoken to her yet.

Her mum frowned. "I'm not sure that's a good idea, Kim."

"Why not?" Kim persisted. At least it would give her and Caitlin something in common to talk about, she thought.

Kim's mum hesitated before she spoke. "I told you that Caitlin seems quite young for her age. Well, that's because her mum wraps her up in cotton-wool quite a bit. She worries about her, and I'm not sure she'd want Caitlin to go horse-riding."

"We could ask her," Kim pointed out.

"Maybe." Kim's mum shot her a warning look. "But if she says no, you're not to interfere, Kim!"

"As if I would!" Kim sniffed as her mum swung the car up a large, tree-lined drive. "Is this the hotel? Wow! It's cool!"

The hotel was a huge stone building with sweeping, landscaped gardens front and back, and a large conservatory built on the side which served as a dining-room. Kim was even more thrilled when she saw the bedroom where she and her mother were staying. It wasn't enormous, but it had a balcony which had a gorgeous view over the floodlit back garden, and a very cosy double bed she was going to share with her mother.

"This is great, Mum!" Kim announced, bouncing up and down enthusiastically on the bed. "I'm so glad I came!"

"Well, go and have a wash and comb your hair before we go for something to eat!" her mum told her, shooing her into the bathroom. "You look like something the cat dragged in!"

Kim felt as if she was living in some kind of fairytale world when she and her mum went down to the brightly-lit conservatory for their evening meal. She could smell lots of delicious food smells, and her mouth was watering.

"Melissa wants us to sit with Caitlin and her tutor," said Kim's mum as they walked past all the tables where people were sitting, eating and chatting. "So remember, young lady, best behaviour please!"

Kim nodded. "OK."

Caitlin and the scary-looking Mrs Franklin were sitting at a table beside the glass doors that opened out on to the garden. Melissa Murray and her co-star sat at a large table next-door to them.

"Oh, hello again!" said Melissa Murray, looking

pleased when she caught sight of the Millers. "Kim, why don't you go and sit by Caitlin, then you can get to know each other?"

"All right," said Kim, hoping she sounded more enthusiastic than she actually was. She slid into the seat next to Caitlin and smiled at her. Caitlin immediately turned bright red and gave Kim a half-smile back, trying to grin without showing the braces on her teeth too much.

"What are you having?" Kim asked her.

Caitlin opened her mouth to reply, but she didn't get the chance.

"Oh, Caitlin, I think you should definitely have some salad," Melissa Murray interrupted, leaning over from the neighbouring table. "You're looking a little peaky, honey, and I think you need to get some more vitamins inside you."

"She didn't take her multi-vitamin tablet this morning, Miss Murray," said Mrs Franklin grimly.

"Oh, Caitlin!" said her mother, shaking her head, while Kim watched with her mouth open in amazement.

"I forgot," Caitlin muttered miserably.

"Definitely salad then," her mother said firmly.

"And some mineral water to cleanse your system."

"What are you having, Kim?" Rachel Miller asked.

"Fish and chips, and lemonade," Kim replied firmly. She wasn't having salad and mineral water whatever Melissa Murray said!

By the time the meal was almost over, Kim was wondering how on earth Caitlin could stand her mother and Mrs Franklin fussing over her all the time. She wasn't allowed to do anything or say

anything without one or other of the adults butting in and taking over. It made Kim feel quite indignant, especially when she saw Caitlin casting sidelong glances at Kim's huge plate of fish and chips.

"Well, I think you'd better go for your evening walk before you go to bed, honey," Melissa Murray said, as Caitlin went over to the next door table to say goodnight to her mother. "Just to make sure you don't get indigestion."

"I'll go for a walk with you, Caitlin," Kim said quickly, feeling really sorry for the other girl by now.

"Oh, isn't that sweet of you, Kim!" said the actress with a smile. "Mrs Franklin usually goes walking with Caitlin, but I'm sure they'd just love you to go along."

"I'd rather go with Kim on my own." Caitlin spoke up for herself for the first time since they'd met, and Kim smiled to herself. Maybe Caitlin wasn't such a mouse after all.

"Well, honey, I don't know about that," Melissa Murray said anxiously. "It's real dark out there."

"Oh, we'll just stay in the hotel garden," Kim added, backing Caitlin up. "We'll be fine."

"Well, just for five minutes then," said the actress reluctantly. Kim and Caitlin immediately dived out through the conservatory doors before she could change her mind and before Mrs Franklin could get up and follow them. As soon as they were outside, Kim breathed a sigh of relief.

"I thought we were going to get stuck with that spooky governess of yours!" Then she blushed. "Sorry, I didn't mean to be nasty. But she is a bit scary!"

"Oh, Mrs Franklin's all right," Caitlin replied, scuffing at the grass with her trainers. "She just nags me all the time, that's all!"

"Don't you hate it?" Kim asked sympathetically.

Caitlin shrugged. "I'm used to it," she said in a small voice.

"Don't you go to school?" Kim asked.

"Yeah, but Mum likes me to come with her when she's filming overseas," Caitlin explained. "So then Mrs Franklin comes with us to look after me."

They walked down the floodlit garden towards the large fountain which stood in the middle of it without speaking. Kim was wondering how someone like the daughter of a rich and famous film star could have what seemed to be a pretty miserable life. She just couldn't understand it.

"Your mum—" Kim stopped. She'd been about to say that Caitlin's mum fussed over her all the time, but instead she said: "Your mum worries about you a lot, doesn't she?"

"I guess," Caitlin admitted, staring at the stone fishes in the middle of the fountain which were spouting foaming sprays of water from their mouths.

"Doesn't it drive you mad?" Kim asked bluntly. "It'd send me bananas if my mum did that!"

"Yeah, it does," Caitlin said. "But she only fusses about me because I'm so hopeless at everything."

Kim climbed up on to the narrow ledge that ran around the edge of the fountain, and stared at her. "What? You must be good at *something*!"

"No, I'm hopeless!" Caitlin repeated, watching Kim walk round the ledge slowly and carefully like a tightrope walker. "I can't do anything right."

Kim had an idea. "Have you ever tried horse-riding?"

"Horse-riding!" Caitlin turned pale with fear. "I couldn't – I'm scared of horses!"

"What about Midnight?" Kim asked as Caitlin

clambered up on to the edge of the fountain to join her. "You're not scared of him, are you?"

There wasn't time for Caitlin to answer that question. As she tried to follow Kim by walking along the fountain ledge, her foot slipped – and she toppled head-first into the water.

5

"Caitlin!" Kim gasped in horror. She leaned into the fountain to grab the other girl's hand, praying that she could swim. But it didn't really matter, because as Caitlin came up for air, coughing and spluttering, Kim realised that the water wasn't in fact very deep.

"Are you OK?" Kim asked, trying to haul Caitlin to her feet. "I thought you were drowning!"

"It's only about a metre deep!" Caitlin spluttered. She tried to stand up, staggered and ended up splashing Kim instead.

"Hey, watch it!" said Kim indignantly.

Caitlin grinned and deliberately flicked some more water in Kim's direction.

"You did that on purpose!" Kim yelled, beginning to laugh. She couldn't help it. Caitlin was soaked to the skin, and she looked really funny. Caitlin began to laugh too, even though she was starting to shiver.

"Come on, get out of there!" Kim said between giggles.

"Caitlin! Oh my God, what have you been doing?"

Caitlin stopped laughing immediately as her mother and Mrs Franklin rushed towards them, looking horrified. Kim was dismayed to see that her own mother was right behind them, and she didn't look very pleased either.

"I'm fine, Mum," Caitlin muttered, climbing out of the fountain and shaking herself like a wet puppy.

"You could catch your death of cold!" Melissa Murray wailed. "And thank goodness your tetanus jabs are up to date!"

"That water looks none too clean to me, Miss

Murray," Mrs Franklin observed gloomily.

"I'm fine," Caitlin insisted, but no-one was taking any notice.

"And how on earth did you fall in there anyway, Caitlin?" her mother demanded suspiciously, and she fixed Kim with an accusing gaze.

"It wasn't Kim's fault, Mom!" Caitlin said between coughs.

"Come along, young lady, you're going straight into a nice hot tub!" said Mrs Franklin sternly, and she marched Caitlin off like a prisoner, with Melissa Murray hurrying along beside them. Kim watched them go, and then turned to face her mother.

"Well, that's a good start!" Rachel Miller said ironically. "You've only been here for a few hours, and you've already soaked the star's daughter!"

"It wasn't anything to do with me!" Kim protested. "We were just talking, and Caitlin fell in."

"Just try and be a bit more careful for the rest of the weekend, please, Kim?" her mother sighed. "This job is—"

"Very important, I know!" Kim broke in. "But honestly, Mum, I didn't do anything!"

But that didn't mean to say she *wouldn't* do something if she got the chance, Kim thought silently as she and her mother went back into the hotel. She felt really sorry for Caitlin, and if Kim could help her in any way, she would.

"Hi, are you all right?" Kim asked anxiously as she met Caitlin in the hotel foyer the following morning. Melissa Murray and Midnight were both involved in the filming that morning, and they both had to be on set for 7am sharp, so Kim had had to get up at the same time as her mum.

"I'm fine," Caitlin said with a huge yawn. "Mom wanted me to stay in bed today, but there's nothing wrong with me! Are you going to the set?"

"Yeah, but we're going to pick Midnight up from the stables first."

"Do *you* like horses?" Caitlin asked shyly.

Kim nodded. "Yes, although I've never learnt to ride. I'm having my first lesson this afternoon."

"Are you?" Caitlin looked admiringly at her. "You're so brave!"

"No, I'm not!" Kim scoffed. "Look, why don't you come too?"

"But I told you last night, I'm scared of

63

horses!" Caitlin said helplessly.

"Why?" Kim asked bluntly. "Have you ever been bitten by one?"

"No," Caitlin admitted.

"So what are you scared of?" Kim shrugged. "Look, if you try it once and you don't like it, you don't have to do it again."

Caitlin still didn't look very convinced.

"Look," Kim persisted, "Why don't you come to the stables with us to pick up Midnight? Then you can see some of the horses before we go to the set."

"Well, all right," Caitlin said at last. "I'll have to ask my mom though."

"Caitlin!" Frowning, Melissa Murray swept down the stairs towards them. "I wish you wouldn't wander off without telling me where you're going, honey."

"Mom, is it OK if I travel to the set today with Kim and her mother?" Caitlin asked diffidently.

"What, you mean you don't want to come with us as usual?" her mother asked, as Mrs Franklin tramped down the stairs behind her.

Caitlin shook her head. "Please, Mom."

"Well, I guess it's OK." Melissa Murray cast a

suspicious look at Kim, and forced a smile. "But no more getting into mischief!"

"I promise," Caitlin said solemnly. She watched her mother and governess go out, and then she and Kim both heaved a sigh of relief.

"Mum, Caitlin wants to travel to the set with us this morning, if that's OK," Kim said as Rachel Miller came down the stairs, yawning and pulling on her jacket. "She's asked her mum's permission."

"Fine. We'd better get going though, we've got to pick up Midnight on the way."

Kim saw Caitlin swallow hard, although she didn't actually say anything. She really *was* scared of horses! Well, maybe Kim could help her to get over that . . .

They drove through the morning mist along the valley and down the lane to Greyfriars Stables. Although it was so early, the stablehands were already busy in the courtyard, cleaning out the horses, and Tom Grayson had Midnight all ready for them.

"He's such a big horse!" Caitlin muttered, keeping well behind Kim as they all got out of the car. "That's why he's so scary!"

"Yeah, but we wouldn't be learning to ride on horses like Midnight!" Kim pointed out. "We'd be on little ponies like those." And she pointed at a tubby little grey pony which was just being led out of its stall by one of the stablehands.

"Oh!" said Caitlin, looking a little less nervous. "But they can still bite, can't they?" She leapt backwards then, looking alarmed, as Midnight snorted, tossed his mane and pawed at the ground a few times. "What's he doing that for?"

"He's fine," Kim said impatiently, fishing in her pocket for a sugar lump. "Look, watch this." She held out her hand and Midnight leaned down and took the sugar gently in his mouth. "Now you have a go."

"Me!" Caitlin gasped. "I couldn't!"

Kim ignored her and put a sugar-lump in her hand. "Hold your hand like this," she told her. "Keep it flat."

Caitlin did as she was told, even though she was shaking with fear. Again Midnight dipped his head to take the sugar, and Caitlin gasped as it disappeared.

"Gee, he was so gentle! I didn't feel his teeth at all!"

"There you are!" said Kim triumphantly, patting Midnight on his dark, gleaming neck. "And now you can stroke him."

This time Caitlin looked much less scared. She patted Midnight just as Kim was doing, and then looked enormously pleased with herself. Kim's mum and Tom Grayson, who had been chatting, stopped to watch what was going on.

"Do you want to see one of his tricks?" Kim asked, and Caitlin nodded eagerly. "Go and stand in front of him then."

Caitlin obediently moved to stand in front of Midnight, although she still looked a bit wary.

"Say hello, Midnight!" Kim instructed the horse, and Midnight immediately raised his leg and offered his hoof to Caitlin. Caitlin looked astounded, but took it gingerly and shook it.

"That's so neat!" she said, her eyes wide. "He's so clever!"

"I think Midnight's shown off quite enough for now!" said Kim's mother, leading the horse towards the horse-box. "We'd better get off to the set."

"Do you like horses, Caitlin?" Tom Grayson asked as they all climbed back into the car.

"Um – well, yes, I think I do now!" Caitlin said breathlessly, and Kim grinned.

"If you want to come for a riding lesson with Kim this afternoon, you're very welcome," Tom told her as he checked to make sure the horse-box was properly fastened. "You don't need anything special to wear, jeans and a sweatshirt, and some leather boots will do. We can lend you a hard hat."

"Oh!" Caitlin's eyes lit up. "Yes, I will! Thank you!"

"If your mum says it's all right," Rachel Miller said firmly.

Caitlin's face fell a little, but she nodded. Kim could guess what she was thinking though. Caitlin had about as much chance of being allowed to ride as Kim had of being best mates with Charlotte Appleby.

6

"How do you teach Midnight to do those tricks, Mrs Miller?" Caitlin asked, as they drove off down the lane.

"Well I started off training him with a clicker," Kim's mum replied. "It's a little toy that makes a clicking sound, and you click it every time the animal does exactly what you want it to do."

"I don't get it." Caitlin looked puzzled.

"Well, as soon as you've clicked, you give the animal a food reward," Rachel Miller explained.

"Then they soon catch on that every time they hear the clicker, they're going to get food. And in order to get that magic click, they have to keep on doing the same action! Then once they've learned that, you can teach them verbal and hand signals for the same tricks."

"It sounds real interesting," said Caitlin.

"It is!" Kim told her. "I want to be an animal trainer myself when I grow up."

When they reached the set, everything was in full swing as usual. Because it was so early no-one had had time for any breakfast, so the catering trailer was doing a brisk trade in coffee and bacon and eggs. Kim's mum sent the two girls over to grab themselves something to eat, while she went to report to the assistant directors.

"Do you think your mum will let you come riding this afternoon?" Kim asked as they collected orange juice and fried egg sandwiches, and went to sit on the grass together.

"I don't know," Caitlin muttered, looking rather depressed. "I'll have to ask her."

"Caitlin!" Melissa Murray's voice floated across the set. She was standing on the steps of her private trailer, frowning at them. "Don't sit on the wet grass, honey. You might catch a chill."

Caitlin sighed and got to her feet. Kim shrugged and did the same. She wasn't at all convinced that Caitlin's mum would let her daughter go horse-riding that afternoon. It seemed to Kim that Melissa Murray didn't allow her daughter to do *anything*. It just wasn't fair.

The rehearsals that morning kicked off with a scene between Melissa Murray's character, Kate, and Callum Scott, the actor who was playing her brother, Gwyn. They were arguing over Kate's plans to emigrate to the States to make her fortune, leaving her family behind. Halfway through their argument Midnight as the ghost horse would suddenly appear on the hillside in front of them, but only Kate was able to see it. Kim and Caitlin found themselves a quiet spot down by the lake where they could sit and watch the rehearsals, while Mrs Franklin sat close by with her knitting, keeping a sharp eye on them.

"Doesn't she ever leave you alone?" Kim whispered to Caitlin.

"No, she's kind of like my bodyguard!" Caitlin whispered back "Ssh, the rehearsal's starting."

The assistant directors and Curtis Bernard

were all watching intently as Melissa Murray and Callum Scott prepared for their scene. The early morning sun was just breaking through the clouds, and the director wanted to capture the effect of the sunrise reflected in the waters of the lake.

"Action!"

"You can't mean to leave all this behind, Katie!" Gwyn said, indicating the green valley with a sweep of his arm. "And for what? An unknown world where anything might happen."

"It's a challenge, Gwyn!" said Kate, her eyes shining. "I can make something of my life over there, I know I can!"

"You could make something of your life here too."

"It's not the same." Kate stopped suddenly and shaded her eyes, looking across the valley. "What's that? Up there on the hillside?"

Gwyn looked in the direction she was pointing. "I can't see anything."

"There!" Kate clutched her arm. "It's the black horse!"

Actually, Midnight wasn't on the hillside. He was standing well away from the set with Rachel

Miller, so that he didn't disturb the rehearsals by snorting or stamping his foot at the wrong moment: Kim knew that the scene of the horse standing on the hillside would be filmed separately, and cut into the argument between Gwyn and Kate when the film was edited.

"There's nothing there, Katie!" her brother told her impatiently. "You're seeing things."

"Cut!"

"When are you going to ask your mum if you can come horse-riding?" Kim asked Caitlin, as the director went over to have a word with the two stars.

"I'll ask her later," Caitlin said evasively, and Kim frowned. Caitlin didn't sound too hopeful.

After a few more rehearsals and several takes, the scene between Kate and her brother was finally filmed. There were several more scenes involving other members of Kate's family, and then it was Midnight's turn. He had several scenes to shoot, including the shots which would be edited into the argument scene.

"He's so beautiful!" Caitlin said admiringly as Kim's mother led the horse into position on the hillside, and took off his reins. "I wish I could ride him."

"Maybe you will, one day," Kim replied.

The set fell silent as Kim's mother positioned herself carefully out of the range of the cameras, but so that the horse could see her in the distance. As one of the assistant directors called "Action!", Rachel Miller raised her hand and gave Midnight his cue to gallop towards her. As he came closer towards the marks on the grass where the director wanted him to pause, Kim's mum signalled to him to stop. Midnight immediately slowed to a trot, and then stopped, shaking his mane back and standing quite still.

"Well, I think that's us done for today!" Rachel Miller looked very pleased as she led Midnight over to Caitlin and Kim at the end of the morning. "Midnight's done a great job!"

"He's brilliant!" Caitlin announced, and this time she didn't need any encouragement to give Midnight a big hug. "He's the best horse in the whole world!"

"Caitlin, honey!" A familiar voice drifted across the set towards them, as Melissa Murray headed over to her trailer. "Make sure you wash your hands after you've been petting that animal, dear."

"We'd better get going," Kim's mum said, picking up her bag. "Midnight needs a good rub-down and something to eat. Caitlin, have you asked your mum yet about the riding lessons?"

Caitlin blushed. "No. I'll do it now." And she headed off across the set to her mother's trailer.

"I bet she's not allowed to come," Kim muttered, stroking Midnight's thick black mane.

"Well, if she isn't, she isn't." Her mum shrugged. "There's nothing we can do about it."

But Kim was in for a surprise. A few moments later, Caitlin came running over to them, a smile on her face.

"She said yes!" she panted. "Can we go now?"

"As soon as I've got Midnight settled in his box." Rachel Miller led the horse away as Kim stared at Caitlin, who looked pale but excited.

"Your mum really doesn't mind?"

"No, I told you." Caitlin turned pink. "Come on, let's go." And she turned and walked off after Kim's mother.

Kim shrugged and followed her. She was glad that Caitlin was allowed to finally do something, but she had been sure that Melissa Murray wouldn't allow her daughter to go. It was all a bit weird. Still, Kim wasn't going to worry about it.

When they arrived at Greyfriars Stables, there was already a small group of children there, waiting for the riding lesson to begin. While Kim's mum took charge of making Midnight comfortable in his stall, Tom Grayson took Kim and Caitlin over to join the group. Caitlin looked excited, although Kim couldn't help noticing that she was a bit jumpy, as if she was worried about something. Maybe she was still a bit nervous about learning to ride, Kim decided.

"Hello, everyone," said Tom Grayson, raising his voice so that the whole group could hear him. "Welcome to Greyfriars Stables for your first riding lesson – which hopefully will be the start of many more. Before you get on to a horse, though, there are a few things you need to know."

Kim listened with interest as Tom began by telling them a few facts about horses, and giving them some tips on things to watch out for. Caitlin was also listening intently, her eyes fixed on Tom the whole time he was talking. Then the grey pony that Kim had seen the day before, and which was

called Penny, was brought out of its stall. Tom then showed them how to put a bridle on called a snaffle, which fitted around the pony's head, how to fit and adjust the saddle properly and the correct way to mount and dismount.

"Right, that's enough talking!" Tom said with a grin. "It's about time we gave you the chance to see what riding's all about for yourself! Caitlin, do you want to have a go at getting on to Penny?"

Caitlin turned bright red. Kim thought she was going to say no at first, but then she nodded.

"Right, remember what I told you," Tom instructed her calmly, holding Penny firmly by her reins. "Hold the stirrup in your right hand, and put your left foot into it."

Looking very determined, Caitlin did exactly as she was told as Kim held her breath. She was just pulling herself up and over into the saddle, when a car screeched to a halt outside the stables, and a furious voice yelled "Caitlin! Get down off that animal *at once*!"

7

At the sound of her mother's voice, Caitlin gave a gasp of horror and slipped. She tumbled off the pony, and landed on her bottom on the courtyard. Kim immediately grabbed her and hauled her to her feet, as Melissa Murray climbed out of her chauffeur-driven car and dashed over to them.

"*Caitlin*! What on earth are you doing!" she shouted. "You could have been badly hurt!"

"I'm fine, Mom," Caitlin muttered, rubbing her backside, while Kim bit her lip, feeling frustrated.

She was sure that if Caitlin's mother hadn't turned up and put her daughter off as usual, Caitlin would have been able to get on to Penny, no problem.

"No bones broken, Miss Murray," said Tom Grayson cheerfully. Everyone else in the courtyard had recognised Melissa Murray by now and they were standing around staring at her. "Everyone takes a tumble now and then when they're learning to ride!"

The actress stared at him in amazement. "Caitlin's learning to *ride*?"

"Well, yes," Tom Grayson looked puzzled.

"She asked you if she could come riding with me, and you said yes," Kim piped up, determined to defend Caitlin.

Caitlin cleared her throat a few times and blushed as her mother turned to look at her.

"I said *what*?"

Kim suddenly realised with a sinking heart that Caitlin obviously *hadn't* asked her mum if she could go riding. She'd just sneaked off without permission. Well, that was probably the first and last riding lesson she'd ever have, judging by the look on Melissa Murray's face.

"What's going on?" Kim's mum came out of Midnight's stall, dusting her hands off.

"Caitlin did *not* have permission to go riding with Kim today," Melissa Murray remarked icily. She was about to say something more, and then as she saw all the stablehands and children staring at her, she thought better of it. "Caitlin, come with me. We're going back to the hotel right now."

Caitlin glanced miserably at Kim, as she handed her borrowed hard hat to one of the stablehands. Then she trailed off after her mother who was marching back to the car where Mrs Franklin was standing by the passenger door, looking very stern indeed.

"Kim! Did you know anything about this?" her mum asked suspiciously, drawing Kim aside as Tom Grayson resumed his lesson.

"No, of course not!" Kim said indignantly. "Caitlin *said* she'd asked her mum, and I believed her."

"She must have guessed her mum would say no," said Rachel Miller. "So she wasn't taking any chances! It was a very silly thing to do though."

"And now Melissa Murray thinks we're to blame!" Kim said gloomily. She'd seen the look

Caitlin's mum had given her before they left. The actress obviously thought it was Kim's fault that Caitlin had disobeyed her.

"I know." Kim's mother looked grim. "We'll talk about this later. You'd better go back to the others. You're missing your lesson."

Kim went back to join the beginners group, but she still couldn't help thinking about Caitlin. It was about time the poor girl was allowed to have some fun, Kim thought, and she was determined to help her in any way she could.

"So what do you think?" Rachel Miller asked as Kim climbed into the car. "Do you like riding or not?"

"I loved it!" Kim said enthusiastically. "Ouch!" She rubbed her bottom as she lowered herself gingerly down on to the seat. "I'm sore all over though!"

"Think what the poor pony must be like then!" her mum said teasingly. "I saw you bouncing up and down on her back all over the field!"

"It was a good laugh!" Kim said with a grin. "But it would've been even better if Caitlin was there."

Her mother shot her a warning glance. "Kim, just leave it, all right?"

"But it's not fair," Kim persisted. "Caitlin's mum doesn't let her do *anything*."

"Yes, I know she's just a little over-protective," Kim's mother agreed as she drove along the valley. "But it's only because she worries about her so much."

"Yeah, but that makes Caitlin worse," Kim pointed out. "She gets really nervous about everything because her mum fusses all the time."

"Kim, I really don't want you to get involved," her mother said firmly. "In fact, I think you should keep a pretty low profile from now on until your dad picks you up on Monday evening."

"But, Mum—" Kim began.

"No buts, Kim." Her mum swung the car into the hotel car park. "I'm as sorry for Caitlin as you are, but we can't interfere. Melissa is her mother, after all. And *Animal Stars* really needs this job to go smoothly."

"You mean I can't be friends with Caitlin any more?" Kim asked in a small voice.

Her mother hesitated. "I think you should keep away from her tonight at least, and give

Melissa a chance to cool down."

Kim didn't say anything as they got into the lift and went up to their room. But she was thinking hard.

"I'm going to jump in the shower," her mum said as she unlocked the door. "You can watch TV if you like."

"Can I go down to the hotel reception and buy some postcards?" Kim asked. "I want to send one to Sarah."

Her mother laughed. "You'll see her before she gets it! Well, go on, if you want to, but come straight back."

Kim grinned, and went off towards the stairs. But she didn't go down to the hotel reception. Instead she ran up to the next floor, where she knew Caitlin, her mother and her governess were staying in a suite of rooms.

Feeling a bit nervous, Kim went over to the door, and knocked. After a few seconds Mrs Franklin opened the door. She stared down her nose at Kim without smiling.

"Yes?" she asked with a frown.

"Can I speak to Caitlin please?" Kim said bravely.

"Caitlin is in bed, recovering from her ordeal at the moment," Mrs Franklin replied.

"What ordeal?" Kim asked, puzzled. "Oh, you mean falling off the horse!"

"Yes, and she can't be disturbed. We'll be dining up here tonight." And Mrs Franklin shut the door in Kim's face.

"What a cheek!" Kim said indignantly to herself as she went back down the stairs. "Poor old Caitlin!"

"You're very quiet, Kim," her mother said as they sat at their table in the conservatory, eating a meal later that evening. "What's the matter?"

"I was thinking about Caitlin," Kim muttered, digging her spoon into a huge Knickerbocker Glory.

"Well, they've not come down to dinner tonight, so I think Melissa must still be mad at us!" Rachel Miller remarked dryly.

"Yeah, she probably wishes she'd never invited me down here!" Kim said. "You don't think she might tell you to send me home, do you, Mum?"

"I doubt it," her mother replied. "You're going home in a day or two anyway."

Kim nodded gloomily. She might not even get the chance to speak to her new friend again before she left, if Melissa Murray and Mrs Franklin were determined to keep them apart. Kim sighed, stared out into the garden and ate another spoonful of ice-cream. As she swallowed it, though, she nearly choked. Someone had popped out from behind one of the trees, and was waving madly at her. It was Caitlin!

Kim dropped her spoon immediately. "Mum, I think left my baseball cap out in the garden the other night. Can I go and look for it?"

"All right," her mother said, sipping her coffee. "But keep away from that fountain!"

Kim hurried out into the garden, and rushed over to where Caitlin was waiting for her.

"How on earth did you get out?" Kim whispered, grabbing her arm. "I thought you were supposed to be in bed!"

"I was," Caitlin gasped, looking as if she'd scared herself silly by doing something so daring. "But Mum was having a bath, and Mrs Franklin went into her room to watch TV, so I sneaked out! I can't stay long though."

"I tried to come and see you this afternoon," Kim told her, "but that old dragon wouldn't let me in!"

"I know." Caitlin hung her head. "My mum's told her to keep me away from you from now on."

"Why?" Kim wanted to know.

"She says I've been behaving really badly since I met you!" Caitlin looked even more embarrassed. "She says you're a bad influence!"

"What a cheek!" Kim gasped.

"I know, it wasn't your fault I sneaked off to go riding," Caitlin gabbled desperately. "I knew Mum would say no, so I just told her I was getting a lift back to the hotel with you and your mum. Then someone on the set mentioned to her that we were going riding, and she came after me."

"It was a shame you couldn't stay," Kim said. "It was a real laugh."

"I bet," Caitlin said wistfully. "I still really want to learn, you know."

"You should talk to your mum," Kim began. But Caitlin just looked hopelessly at her and shook her head.

"Look, you'd better go," Kim told her. "I'll see you tomorrow."

Caitlin looked even more unhappy. "I don't think so. Mum says I've got to stay in her trailer all day tomorrow to make sure I've recovered from my fall."

"To make sure you keep away from me, you mean!" said Kim, trying to make a joke of it. "Does she treat all your friends this way?"

Caitlin looked down at her feet. "I don't have that many friends anyway," she muttered, and hurried away.

Kim stared after her, feeling quite upset. She couldn't just do what her mum and Melissa Murray wanted, and leave Caitlin alone, because

Caitlin obviously needed a friend. Kim wasn't going to let her down either, whatever her mother said about not interfering. She was going to do something about it – even if it meant a showdown with one of the most famous film stars in the world!

8

The black horse was galloping through the white plumes of mist which were curling and twisting around him. Then something startled him, and he stopped, rearing up on to his back legs and tossing his head.

"Cut! That was great!" called the director.

Kim sat on her own at the side of the set, and watched her mum slip a halter over Midnight's neck and lead him away. The horse was performing brilliantly, as usual. The morning's shooting involved several scenes of Midnight galloping free along the hills, his mane flying, and Kim thought it would look very effective on the screen. She just hoped that Caitlin was watching from the trailer, although it was parked quite a distance away from where this particular piece of action was being shot.

Kim hadn't seen Caitlin since the previous night. Midnight hadn't had to be on set until later that afternoon, but Melissa Murray had got in earlier, so Caitlin and her mother were already on set by the time Kim had got there. Although Melissa Murray had been in the middle of rehearsing a scene when the Millers and Midnight had got to the set, Caitlin was nowhere to be seen. She was obviously not going to be allowed out of the trailer that afternoon.

"I wonder where Caitlin is?" Kim's mum remarked as she led Midnight over to where Kim was standing.

"She's in the trailer," Kim replied without thinking. "She's not allowed to talk to me any more – her mum thinks I'm a bad influence!"

Rachel Miller raised her eyebrows. "Oh? And when did you find *that* out?"

Kim was caught. "Caitlin told me," she muttered.

"Really." Her mother's eyes bored into Kim's. "I didn't think you'd seen Caitlin since the riding lesson yesterday."

Kim squirmed guiltily. "I saw her last night. She sneaked out when her mum and the old dragon – I mean Mrs Franklin – weren't looking."

"Kim, do you ever listen to a word I say?" her mother snapped. "I told you not to interfere!"

"Well, I couldn't not talk to her!" Kim pointed out hotly, her quick temper flaring instantly. "I'm about the only friend she's got!"

"I'm sure that's not true," her mother began.

"It is!" Kim insisted. "I can't help feeling sorry for her."

Rachel Miller sighed. "I know you're only trying to help, Kim, but you've just got to mind your own business, I'm afraid. Caitlin has to work out her problems with her mother on her own." She tethered Midnight firmly to a nearby fence post. "We've only got one more scene to do this afternoon, and then we're done here. What time's your riding lesson?"

"Five o'clock," Kim muttered. Her bottom

wasn't quite so sore today, and she was looking forward to getting on to a pony again, but it would be much more fun if Caitlin was coming too.

"OK, we'll have time to go back to the hotel for some tea first." Her mum glanced at Kim's sulky face. "We've got a night shoot tonight, so there'll be lots of ghostly shots of Midnight galloping through the darkness!"

"Great," Kim muttered.

Her mum sighed, and handed her a large bucket. "Go and get Midnight some fresh water from the catering trailer, will you?"

Kim took the bucket and stomped off, still feeling furiously angry. She hadn't even done anything, and she kept on getting blamed for everything Caitlin did! Just because Caitlin had started standing up to her mother a little at last, Melissa Murray thought that Kim was a bad influence. Well, it was about time someone told her a thing or two!

Kim was so angry by now that she didn't stop to think twice about what she was doing. She stormed over to Melissa Murray's trailer, and dropped the bucket at the bottom of the steps.

Then she marched up to the door, and knocked on it.

A second later Caitlin opened it and her face lit up. "Kim!"

"Hi!" Kim said quickly. "Do you want to come over to the catering trailer with me? I need to get some water for Midnight."

Caitlin opened her mouth to reply, but before she could do so, Mrs Franklin loomed up behind them like a prison jailer.

"Come inside at once, Caitlin!" she said sharply. "You know your mother wants you to rest up today."

"But I'm fine," Caitlin answered. "I want to go with Kim."

"We'll only be five minutes," Kim chimed in, determined not to let Mrs Franklin scare her off.

"What's going on out here?" Melissa Murray came over to the trailer door, wearing a pink silk dressing-gown and an eye mask which she'd pushed up on top of her head. She saw Kim and gave her an icy stare. "Oh, it's you."

"I just came to see Caitlin," Kim said defiantly, refusing to be cowed, even though she couldn't help feeling a bit nervous.

"Caitlin isn't up to seeing anyone today," said Melissa Murray coldly. "She's still recovering from yesterday."

"She only fell off a horse!" said Kim. "She didn't even hurt herself!"

"No, I didn't!" Caitlin said bravely. "And I still want to learn to ride!"

Melissa Murray looked stunned, as if no-one had ever dared to disagree with her before. "Caitlin, I'm your mother and you'll do what I say!" she snapped. "Now come inside and shut the door!" She put a hand up to her face. "I'm getting one of my headaches. I'm not sure I'll be able to do my scenes this afternoon."

"That's because you've been upset, Miss Murray," said Mrs Franklin, glancing accusingly at Kim. "Come along, I'll find your painkillers. And Caitlin, shut the door."

Caitlin did as she was told, but before she did so she leaned out and whispered to Kim, "Are you coming to the night shoot tonight?"

Kim nodded.

"I'm going to make Mom take some notice of me for once!" Caitlin said in a determined voice. "I've got a great idea!"

"Caitlin, shut that door AT ONCE!"

Caitlin quickly obeyed, leaving Kim standing on the step, frowning. It looked as if, with Kim's help, Caitlin was finally beginning to stand up for herself. But Kim couldn't help worrying about what Caitlin's great idea was. She just hoped it wasn't something which would get them both into even more serious trouble . . .

"Right, Kim, make sure you behave yourself tonight," her mother warned her as they made their way over to the set that evening. "You know how difficult night shoots can sometimes be, and I don't want to be worrying about you all the time."

"OK," Kim agreed, trying to look innocent, but panicking secretly underneath. She hadn't seen Caitlin since that morning, so she still had no idea what the other girl was planning.

The set was a blaze of light within the pitch-black circle of the hills that surrounded the valley. It was a very cold, clear night, and the dark sky was studded with tiny stars. Everyone who was running around organising the equipment ready for the filming to start was well wrapped up, and

Kim was glad she'd brought her gloves and scarf as well as her baseball cap with her.

"Kim!" As Kim stood on her own while her mother attended to Midnight, she heard a low voice calling her name from behind the catering trailer. Kim spun round immediately.

"Caitlin!"

"I haven't got much time," Caitlin gabbled. "Mom's talking to Mr Bernard in the trailer, and I just said I was going to get a hot chocolate and ran off!"

Kim quickly slipped behind the trailer to join her. "What's your great idea then?"

"Well, I thought if Mom could see that I really like horses," Caitlin explained breathlessly, "she might let me try out riding lessons again."

Kim thought that was a pretty slim hope, but she didn't say so.

"So I thought if she could just see me getting along real well with Midnight," Caitlin went on, "she might change her mind."

"So what are you going to do?" Kim asked.

"Well, I thought maybe your mum would let me get up on his back," Caitlin said eagerly.

Kim stared at her. "Are you kidding? Midnight's

a horse, not a pony! Besides, he hasn't got a saddle on or anything!"

"So?" Caitlin stared defiantly back at her. "I don't have to *go* anywhere. Just sit there, just to show Mom I'm not scared."

"Forget it! My mum won't let you do it in a million years," Kim said with conviction. "First off, she's be worried about you getting hurt, and second, Midnight's a really valuable horse. Mum's got to be really careful with him."

Caitlin's lips trembled. "Well, I've got to do something!" she muttered tearfully, and then she turned and dashed away.

Kim sighed. Maybe she hadn't been very helpful, but Caitlin's idea was crazy! She certainly wasn't an experienced enough rider to even think of getting up on to a big horse like Midnight, and if she happened to have an accident, Melissa Murray would throw a fit.

The assistant directors were bustling around now, getting everyone ready for the first rehearsal of the night. Then Melissa Murray emerged from her trailer, a large, fluffy fake fur coat over her costume, and joined the other actors and actresses on the set.

"Have you seen Caitlin?" Kim heard Melissa Murray ask Mrs Franklin in a worried voice. "She went to get a hot drink, but she hasn't come back yet."

"I'll go look for her right away," Mrs Franklin said. "She can't have gone far."

"I just hope she's not with that dreadful girl—" Melissa Murray began, then stopped as she saw Kim looking at her. "Come and tell me the minute you find her."

Kim hoped Caitlin hadn't done something silly, like running away from the set. It would be easy to get lost in the hills, especially in the dark.

"Looks like there might be a mist coming down," Rachel Miller remarked, coming over to Kim as the actors and actresses began to move into position. "That'll please Curtis! We won't need the dry ice machines at this rate!"

Kim hadn't noticed, but now she looked around and saw thin swirls of white most curling around the hilltops. "What if it gets really foggy?" she asked.

"We stop filming, and Curtis goes bananas!" her mum said with a grin. She picked up her large shoulder bag, which Kim had been looking after, and began rooting in it. "Kim, have you seen my scarf? It's freezing out here."

"No." Kim was beginning to feel cold too, and she stamped her feet up and down in an attempt to keep warm. Then she glanced across the set to where Midnight was tethered safely to one side, warmly wrapped up in his blanket until it was time for filming to start. Kim's heart missed a beat. Caitlin was climbing up on to the fence right next to the horse, and she'd already undone Midnight's blanket and let it slip to the ground. The crew and the actors were so intent on preparing for the scene that no-one was taking any notice, except Kim.

"What is she *doing*!" Kim muttered. Surely Caitlin wasn't going to attempt to climb up on to Midnight's back? But it looked like she was. Midnight was obviously becoming uneasy, and was moving around quite a lot, making it difficult for Caitlin to climb on. Kim didn't know what to do. She couldn't call out in case she startled either Caitlin or Midnight, and if she did alert everyone, Caitlin would be in serious trouble. Then Kim's heart lurched. Unable to get on to the horse in the position she was in, Caitlin was struggling to untie the animal from the post where he was tethered. Kim panicked immediately. Caitlin obviously had no idea how strong the horse was – Kim knew for sure that she would never be able to control him!

"Mum!" Kim grabbed her mother's arm. "Look!"

In the split-second it took Rachel Miller to glance up and see what was going on, Caitlin finally released Midnight. Although she tried desperately to hang on to the reins, Midnight sensed that something wasn't quite right. He reared back, jerking the reins from Caitlin's hand, and ran. Next moment he had disappeared towards the hills, invisible in the inky darkness.

9

For a moment everyone on set was too shocked to move except for Kim's mum. She immediately raced off in the direction the horse had gone, pulling a torch out of her pocket, and whistling and calling out to Midnight in a reassuring tone. Kim stood where she was, frozen to the spot, her heart hammering. No-one else on the set had seen that Caitlin was involved – all they'd seen was the horse bolting, and now they were all talking at the tops of their voices.

"This is all we need!" Curtis Bernard was roaring. "Let's get some lights trained on this area – see if we can pick this horse up fast!"

"Oh, Caitlin, you idiot!" Kim said to herself. But it just showed how desperate the other girl was to have done such a stupid thing. Caitlin herself was standing by the fence looking completely stricken, as if she'd just realised exactly what she'd done. Then, as Kim watched, she turned and ran off into the darkness.

"Caitlin!"

Without thinking, Kim rushed across the set after her, and down the valley path. There was plenty of light from the set to see by, and she saw Caitlin vanish over the lower slopes of one of the hills. Kim raced after her, stopping for a moment to check exactly where the set was over her shoulder. It was vitally important that they didn't get lost out there in the hills.

As Kim got further away from the set, the light diminished rapidly, and she had to fumble for the torch she had in her pocket. Torches were standard equipment for night shoots, and Kim always brought her own with her. Switching it on, she played it round the hillsides, searching desperately for the other girl and for Midnight.

"Caitlin!" she called. "Caitlin, where are you?" And after five minutes of walking and shouting until she was hoarse, Kim finally heard a faint reply.

"Over here!"

Kim rushed to the spot, and found Caitlin standing shivering in the middle of the hillside, surrounded by sheep.

"What are you doing!" Kim gasped as she rushed over to her. "Why did you run off like that?"

Caitlin hung her head. "I wanted to find Midnight. It was my fault he ran off."

"I know, I saw." Kim took her hand and held it firmly. She didn't want Caitlin charging off again. "Look, don't worry, Mum'll find him. He won't go far."

"I'm glad you've got a torch," Caitlin said, clinging to her hand. "I think I bumped into a sheep!" She shivered. "It's so dark out here!"

"Yeah, well, there aren't any street lamps out in the hills!" Kim said with a shaky grin. She'd be glad to get back to the flood-lit set herself. "Come on, I think I remember the way back."

She turned round confidently, and then stopped, horrified. A thick white fog was sweeping down from the hilltops, towards them, totally obscuring the view in front of them.

"Are you sure you can find the set?" Caitlin asked nervously.

Kim swallowed hard. She could barely make out anything in front of them. "I thought I could," she said in a small voice. "But that was before the mist came down."

"What are we going to do?" Caitlin asked, her teeth chattering with cold and fear.

"Maybe we ought to wait here for someone to come and find us," Kim said, wondering how long that would be. She was pretty sure that her mum would have recaptured Midnight by now – the horse was too well-trained to have gone very far. Surely by now someone would have noticed that she and Caitlin were missing? "If we try to find our way back in this fog, we could end up getting even more lost."

"Oh!" Caitlin suddenly clutched Kim's arm so tightly that Kim winced. "Look! What's *that*?"

Kim strained her eyes to see through the mist, and her stomach turned over with fear. A large

107

black shape was looming through the mist towards them, coming closer and closer.

Both girls were too scared even to scream. They stared at the black shadow as it came closer and closer, and then suddenly they heard a soft neighing sound.

"It's Midnight!" Kim cried out with relief, and sure enough, a swirl of mist cleared away just long enough to give the two girls a glimpse of the black horse. Midnight had stopped a little distance away from them, and was pawing the ground, his eyes fixed on them.

"Come here, Midnight!" Kim said gently, moving towards him, but Midnight shied away, keeping his distance. He stopped again, a little further on, and watched the girls closely.

"He wants us to follow him!" Caitlin said. "Come on, Kim – he'll lead us back to the set!"

"Hang on, we don't know that!" Kim argued.

"He will, I know he will!" Caitlin gasped, and without hesitation she hurried towards the black horse. Kim was forced to go after her, although it was against her better judgement. Midnight might lead them right out into the hills, and then they'd really be in trouble.

The horse trotted on ahead of them, turning every so often as if to check the two girls were following him. Every so often thick fingers of mist would drift across the path, and the horse would disappear from view, but every time the mist cleared, Midnight was always standing there, waiting patiently for them. Then, in the foggy distance, Kim caught a glimpse of blazing lights.

"There's the set!" she gasped, clutching Caitlin's hand. "Come on!"

"What about Midnight?" Caitlin asked,

straining her eyes to catch a glimpse of the horse, who had disappeared into the mist again.

"We'll have to fetch Mum," Kim said urgently. "He won't let us catch him."

The two girls ran towards the set. The mist was beginning to clear a little, and it looked as though filming was still going on.

"Caitlin!" Melissa Murray pounced on her daughter as soon as she and Kim arrived back on set. "Where have you been? I've been going frantic here!"

"Sorry, Mom!" Caitlin gasped. "I had to go to look for Midnight – it was my fault that he disappeared!"

"What?" Caitlin's mother looked bewildered.

"It was me who untied him!" Caitlin gabbled on. "And then I got lost and Kim came to look for me, and Midnight came and found us and he led us back here!"

"And now I've got to find Mum before he runs off again!" Kim added, looking round. And then her eyes widened. Her mother was leading Midnight towards them. The horse looked none the worse for his experience, and was warmly wrapped up in his horse blanket.

"Mum! You found him!" Kim exclaimed in relief.

"Yes, almost straightaway," her mother replied. "He didn't go far, luckily."

Kim and Caitlin looked at each other. "But Midnight's only just come back!" Kim said, bewildered. "Caitlin and me got lost in the hills, and Midnight led us back here."

"That's impossible, Kim!" her mother said with a frown. "I caught Midnight only a minute or two after he got free! And anyway, what on earth were you doing running off the set? You could have got lost!"

Kim wasn't taking any notice of what her mum was saying though. She and Caitlin were staring at each other, speechless. If it hadn't been Midnight who had led them back to safety, who had that mysterious black horse *been*?

10

"It was the ghost horse!" Caitlin breathed, her eyes lighting up. "Do you remember, Kim? It helps people in trouble! It helped *us*!"

"Well, maybe," Kim replied cautiously. She didn't know *what* to believe. It could have been a real horse, maybe one which had escaped from a stables, or it could have been a wild horse – if there *were* any wild horses in Wales. Kim didn't know. All she did know was that if it hadn't been for that horse, whoever it was, she and Caitlin might still be lost in the cold, misty hills.

"Caitlin, honey, what are you talking about?" her mother said impatiently. "And what do you mean, you were the one who untied that horse? I don't believe you would do such a thing!" Her gaze swivelled round accusingly to Kim. "I expect *you* had something to do with it!"

"No, it was me!" Caitlin said firmly, staring her mother straight in the eye. "I told you, I want to learn to ride!"

"Caitlin, we've talked about this already—"

"No, we haven't!" Caitlin interrupted. "You haven't asked me what *I* want to do! You never ask me!"

Melissa Murray looked uncertainly at her daughter, and Kim glanced at Caitlin too. Her chin was up and her face was set. Obviously she was determined to learn to ride, and she was going to make sure her mother knew it!

"Oh, Miss Murray." Mrs Franklin hurried over to them. "The wardrobe department are waiting for you."

"I'll go and change right now," Melissa Murray muttered, still looking rather dazed. "Caitlin, you'd better come with me."

"I just have something to say to Kim first," Caitlin replied, staring steadily at her mother as she stayed where she was. At first Melissa Murray looked as if she was about to say something, but then she just nodded tightly, and went off to her trailer.

"I'm going to put Midnight in the horse-box until his next scene," Kim's mother said with a sigh. "And then you've got some explaining to do, Kimberley Miller!"

"I'm sorry about what happened, Mrs Miller," Caitlin said timidly.

"Well, it was a very silly thing to do, but fortunately there's no harm done." Kim's mother led Midnight away. "I don't know what all this nonsense is about a ghost horse though!"

"It wasn't nonsense, was it?" Caitlin whispered, clutching Kim's arm. "It was magic!"

Kim shrugged. "I just don't know, Caitlin."

"It was!" Caitlin insisted. "It was the most wonderful thing that's ever happened to me!"

Kim stared at her. Caitlin looked so different. Her eyes were shining, her face was glowing and she suddenly looked more alive and much more confident.

"Well, maybe it *was* magic," Kim muttered. Wherever the horse had come from, it had certainly worked some kind of magic on Caitlin!

"Do you know, I can't believe I was ever scared of horses," Caitlin went on. "They're fantastic! And I can't wait to learn how to ride!"

"Do you think your mum will let you?" Kim asked, and Caitlin looked at her in amazement.

"Of course she will!" she said confidently. "I'm just going to have to talk her round!"

"And if you ever do anything like that again, you'll never set foot on a set again!" Rachel Miller said for the fifth time as she and Kim hurried downstairs the next morning. They had finished filming late the night before, so had had a lie-in. Now they were due on set, after picking up Midnight, ready to start filming after lunch.

Kim groaned. "All right, all right, Mum! I've said I'm sorry!"

"Running off into the Welsh hills in the dark was a seriously stupid thing to do," her mum went on as they reached the hotel foyer. "I thought you'd learnt your lesson after that night shoot for

North Park Avenue when Jamie Marshall nearly drowned."

"But nothing like that happened to me and Caitlin!" Kim protested. "We got back safely."

"Yes, but only thanks to that mysterious horse you thought was Midnight." Her mother frowned. "I wonder if it had escaped from a local stables. Maybe I'd better ask Tom Grayson if he knows anyone who's lost a black horse."

"Caitlin thinks it was the ghost horse," Kim muttered.

"Oh, really, Kim!" said her mum with a smile. "Look, there's Caitlin waving at you."

Caitlin, her mother and Mrs Franklin were just coming down the stairs, also on their way to the set. Caitlin was looking just as happy and confident as she had last night, while her mother still seemed slightly stunned as if she couldn't quite believe the change in her quiet, timid daughter. Mrs Franklin was looking on, even more grim-faced than usual.

"Hi, Kim!" Caitlin hurried over to her without waiting for permission. "Can I catch a ride with you and your mom to the set?"

"Sure," Kim said, with a glance at Melissa

Murray to see if she would object, but she didn't.

"Great! See you at the set then, Mom!" And Caitlin gave her mother a big hug, and followed Kim and Rachel out into the car park.

"Is everything OK with you and your mum now?" Kim asked curiously as they climbed into the car.

Caitlin grinned. "We had a long talk last night," she said. "And I think things are going to change a bit from now on! I guess Mom will still fuss a lot, but I'm not going to put up with it like I did before!"

"Good for you!" Kim said admiringly.

"And guess what?" Caitlin went on. "I'm flying back to the States in a couple of days time – I'm going back to school!"

"What about Mrs Franklin?" Kim asked.

"I told Mom that if I had to have someone to look after me on set, I wanted someone real nice!" Caitlin laughed. "No more Mrs Franklin!"

"Your mum must be a bit shocked by all this!" Kim remarked.

"I guess she is," Caitlin admitted. "She even agreed that I could learn to ride!"

"Hey, that's great!" Kim gasped, and she held up her hand for a high five.

"I can start as soon as I get back to school," Caitlin said, slapping Kim's palm with gusto. "Lots of girls in my class have riding lessons."

"Maybe you'll be able to get your own pony," Kim suggested as they pulled into Greyfriars Stables, and Caitlin grinned.

"I don't reckon I can push things that far – yet! I'll just wait and see."

"Will you write to me when you get home?" Kim asked. "Or you can e-mail me if you want."

"Sure," Caitlin agreed eagerly. "And I'll ask Mom if you and your family can come out to visit us too!"

"Cool!" Kim gasped. She was dying to go to America, and it would be brilliant to be able to tell Charlotte Appleby that she was going as Melissa Murray's guest! "You won't forget?"

"I sure won't!" Caitlin said fervently. "You're the best friend I've ever had!"

"See, Mum?" Kim whispered as they all climbed out of the car. "Everything turned out OK in the end!"

"I don't know how you do it, Kim Miller!" her mother replied, shaking her head. "But I wish you wouldn't!"

Kim grinned as Tom Grayson brought Midnight over to them.

"Hello, Midnight!" Caitlin said happily, and gave the horse a sugar-lump without a trace of fear.

"Oh, Tom, have you heard of any horses that have gone missing over the last few days?" Rachel Miller asked, patting Midnight's shining flanks. "There was a black horse which looked like Midnight hanging around the hills near the set last night."

Tom frowned. "No, I've not heard of any horses

on the loose." He grinned. "But it could have been the ghost horse, you know!"

Caitlin nudged Kim.

"It was May 1st, yesterday, wasn't it?" Tom went on. "That's when the ghost horse appears! There are always sightings reported at the beginning of May."

Caitlin grabbed Kim's arm. "You see?" she whispered. "It really *was* the ghost horse who saved us!"

Kim frowned. She didn't really know what to believe. Just who was that beautiful and mysterious black horse which had saved them from getting lost on the cold, misty Welsh hills? It looked like they would never know. But one thing was for sure. Kim would never forget him as long as she lived.

TRIXIE'S MAGIC TRICK
Animal Stars 6

Narinder Dhami

*When Kim Miller's parents start an agency
training animals for TV and film work, she's
delighted. She loves animals and she loves showbiz,
and now Animal Stars is so busy, there's plenty of
opportunity to help out . . .*

Famous magician, Richard Marvel, has asked
Animal Stars to find him ten white rabbits
for a trick in his next big show. There's only
a short time to go, so Kim's mum has her
work cut out for her, especially with naughty
Trixie, the ringleader of the rabbits! Then
the Millers get some shocking news. Richard
has been accused of cruelty to animals. Kim's
sure he's innocent, but can't prove it. Will
the show go on?

ORDER FORM

ANIMAL STARS series
by Narinder Dhami

0 340 74400 6	Animal Stars 1: Harry's Starring Role	£3.50 ☐
0 340 74401 4	Animal Stars 2: Casper in the Spotlight	£3.50 ☐
0 340 74402 2	Animal Stars 3: Spike's Secret	£3.50 ☐
0 340 74403 0	Animal Stars 4: Coco on the Catwalk	£3.50 ☐
0 340 74404 9	Animal Stars 5: Midnight the Movie Star	£3.50 ☐
0 340 74405 7	Animal Stars 6: Trixie's Magic Trick	£3.50 ☐

All Hodder Children's books are available at your local bookshop or newsagent, or can be ordered direct from the publisher. Just tick the titles you want and fill in the form below. Prices and availability subject to change without notice.

Hodder Children's Books, Cash Sales Department, Bookpoint, 39 Milton Park, Abingdon, OXON, OX14 4TD, UK. If you have a credit card you may order by telephone – (01235) 831700.

Please enclose a cheque or postal order made payable to Bookpoint Ltd to the value of the cover price and allow the following for postage and packing:
UK & BFPO – £1.00 for the first book, 50p for the second book, and 30p for each additional book ordered up to a maximum charge of £3.00.
OVERSEAS & EIRE – £2.00 for the first book, £1.00 for the second book, and 50p for each additional book.

Name ....

Address ....

....

If you would prefer to pay by credit card, please complete:
Please debit my Visa/Access/Diner's Card/American Express (delete as applicable) card no:

Signature ....

Expiry Date ....

If you enjoyed this book, why not try the Home Farm Twins series by Jenny Oldfield – about identical twins who are mad about the animals on their Lake District farm!

SAMANTHA THE SNOB
Home Farm Twins Christmas Special

Jenny Oldfield

Meet Helen and Hannah. They're identical twins – and mad about the animals on their Lake District farm!

Samantha, a Cavalier King Charles spaniel, is a Christmas guest at Doveton Manor. Helen and Hannah are looking forward to taking Speckle to meet the little dog, but the snobby, snappy spaniel cuts their beloved sheepdog dead. So, when the precious pooch goes missing, should they even bother to join the search?

HOME FARM TWINS
Jenny Oldfield

66127 5	Speckle The Stray	£3.99	❏
66128 3	Sinbad The Runaway	£3.99	❏
66129 1	Solo The Homeless	£3.99	❏
66130 5	Susie The Orphan	£3.99	❏
66131 3	Spike The Tramp	£3.99	❏
66132 1	Snip and Snap The Truants	£3.99	❏
68990 0	Sunny The Hero	£3.99	❏
68991 9	Socks The Survivor	£3.99	❏
68992 7	Stevie The Rebel	£3.99	❏
68993 5	Samson The Giant	£3.99	❏
69983 3	Sultan The Patient	£3.99	❏
69984 1	Sorrel The Substitute	£3.99	❏
69985 X	Skye The Champion	£3.99	❏
69986 8	Sugar and Spice The Pickpockets	£3.99	❏
69987 6	Sophie The Show-off	£3.99	❏
72682 2	Smoky The Mystery	£3.99	❏
72795 0	Scott The Braveheart	£3.99	❏
72796 9	Spot The Prisoner	£3.99	❏
727977	Shelley The Shadow	£3.99	❏

All Hodder Children's books are available at your local bookshop, or can be ordered direct from the publisher. Just tick the titles you would like and complete the details below. Prices and availability are subject to change without prior notice.

Please enclose a cheque or postal order made payable to *Bookpoint Ltd*, and send to: Hodder Children's Books, 39 Milton Park, Abingdon, OXON OX14 4TD, UK. Email Address: orders@bookpoint.co.uk

If you would prefer to pay by credit card, our call centre team would be delighted to take your order by telephone. Our direct line *01235 400414* (lines open 9.00 am–6.00 pm Monday to Saturday, 24 hour message answering service). Alternatively you can send a fax on *01235 400454*.

TITLE		FIRST NAME		SURNAME	

ADDRESS	

DAYTIME TEL:		POST CODE	

If you would prefer to pay by credit card, please complete:
Please debit my Visa/Access/Diner's Card/American Express (delete as applicable) card no:

Signature .... Expiry Date: ....

If you would NOT like to receive further information on our products please tick the box. ❏